G 10/16

RM. 201

BUYER BEWARE

BY KELLY ROGERS

ILLUSTRATED BY BETSY PETERSCHMIDT

Spellbound

An Imprint of Magic Wagon
abdopublishing.com

For Connor, My adventurer,
who would probably buy an egg, too. —KRP

To my brother Max: for all the years of guidance . . .
and occasional chaos. —BP

abdopublishing.com

Published by Magic Wagon, a division of ABDO, PO Box
398166, Minneapolis, Minnesota 55439. Copyright © 2017 by
Abdo Consulting Group, Inc. International copyrights reserved
in all countries. No part of this book may be reproduced in
any form without written permission from the publisher.
Spellbound™ is a trademark and logo of Magic Wagon.

Printed in the United States of America, North Mankato,
Minnesota.
052016
092016

THIS BOOK CONTAINS
RECYCLED MATERIALS

Written by Kelly Rogers
Illustrated by Betsy Peterschmidt
Edited by Heidi M.D. Elston and Megan M. Gunderson
Designed by Candice Keimig

Library of Congress Cataloging-in-Publication Data

Names: Rogers, Kelly, 1981- author. | Peterschmidt, Betsy, illustrator.

Title: Buyer beware / by Kelly Rogers ; illustrated by Betsy Peterschmidt.

Description: Minneapolis, MN : Magic Wagon, [2017] | Series: Rm. 201 |
   Summary: Ellie buys a snake egg from the sinister science teacher Ms. Fleek in
   room 201, and hides it in a cage in her closet, but when it finally hatches--well,
   snakes are not supposed to have legs and wings, are they?

Identifiers: LCCN 2016002313 (print) | LCCN 2016005836 (ebook) | ISBN
   9781624021671 (lib. bdg.) | ISBN 9781680790467 (ebook)

Subjects: LCSH: Horror tales. | Snakes--Juvenile fiction. | Science teachers--
   Juvenile fiction. | Middle schools--Juvenile fiction. | CYAC: Horror stories. |
   Snakes--Fiction. | Teachers--Fiction. | Middle schools--Fiction. | Schools--Fiction.

Classification: LCC PZ7.1.R65 Bu 2016 (print) | LCC PZ7.1.R65 (ebook) | DDC
   813.6--dc23

LC record available at http://lccn.loc.gov/2016002313

TABLE OF CONTENTS

CHAPTER 1
Eggs for Sale

The sign said "*Snake* Eggs For Sale: $5. See Ms. Fleek." It didn't seem real.

I asked the guys at the bike rack about it. They rolled their eyes. Everyone knows Ms. Fleek is strange.

I had always wanted a pet snake.

I skipped lunch to see Ms. Fleek.

RM. 201 was at the back of the

school. Between the stairs to the

basement and the English

room.

The MONEY was

already in my hand: four

one-dollar bills, plus all

the coins from my

couch.

The lights were turned off. Her room **smelled** like gerbils.

"What do you want, Miss Coe?" she said. Her *eyes* didn't move from her computer.

"I want to buy an **egg**," I said. I did not feel scared, alone in this *smelly* room with Ms. Fleek and her eggs. *I did not.*

"Not yet," she said. "You need a cage. Bedding. A *HEAT* lamp."

It took me two weeks to gather everything. Cage, lamp, and bedding, all *hidden* behind the rarely worn dresses in my closet. I took a picture on my phone of the setup.

The next morning, I rode my bike as **FAST** as I could to school. I couldn't wait to get that egg.

"Here it is," I said, back in

 .

Ms. Fleek looked at me over the
top of her glasses.

"If I give you this egg," she said,
"it's yours for **LIFE**. No returns,
no refunds. Got it?"

"Got it," I said. My **stomach**
tried to send my lunch back up. I
told myself I was just excited.

13

I stopped every few blocks on the way *home*. The egg was fine.

Mom was still at work, so I took the egg straight up to its cage. I made a hole in the bedding. I nestled in the egg. I switched on the heat lamp.

And I began waiting.

Every day for a month, I checked on that egg. I turned it so the **HEAT** got on every part of it. Morning. Night.

But it didn't **hatch**. It didn't get bigger. It just sat there.

CHAPTER 2
Crack!

That changed the third week of October. I woke up to a *thump* from my closet. I tried to go back to sleep, but it *thumped* again.

I sat up. I slipped out of bed. I tiptoed to the closet door. The thing kept **thumping**, louder and louder.

I opened the closet and squeezed
inside. I sat right in front of the cage.

The egg was **hatching**, all right. There weren't any cracks, yet, but it was rolling and rocking. Like it knew. Like it knew once it hatched, it would be **TRAPPED**.

A crack! Now the egg knew what to do. It started **SLAMMING** harder against the side of the cage.

WHAM!

I was scared Mom or my brother, Josh, would wake up.

More **thumping**. More *rolling*.
The eggshell started to fall away.
Just a little at first. That egg kept
on *rolling* until it had shaken off
almost all of the shell.

Something was off about my
snake. Were those . . . hands? I
blinked. It looked right at me. It
had red EYES.

There was a bit of shell still
stuck to its back. I reached my hand
in to get the shell. To *help*.

My snake **SNAPPED** at me! I pulled my hand away and saw blood. That's when I noticed the 𝔴𝔦𝔫𝔤𝔰.

I **backed** out of the closet then. I got back into bed. I kept my eyes on the closet doors. I didn't sleep any more that **NIGHT**.

"No returns, **NO REFUNDS**," Ms. Fleek said when she heard me enter RM. 201.

"No, no," I said. "It's not that. It's just . . . what kind of *snake* is it?"

Ms. Fleek didn't look up.

"You didn't request a *snake* egg," she said.

I **swallowed**. *She was selling other eggs, too?* The bell for class rang. I started to leave.

"Wait," she said. I turned back. "What are you feeding it?"

"Feeding it?" I asked.

She reached underneath her desk, found a jar, and threw it to me.

"Just one a day," she said. "And DON'T open it at school."

After school, I checked on the Thing in its cage. While I was at school, it had built a small hut out of the bedding. I couldn't see the Thing anymore, but I could hear it *breathing*.

I opened the jar from Ms. Fleek. Inside were **slugs** so dark red they were almost black. I used my pencil to pull one out and **drop** it in the cage.

When the slug **FLOPPED** to the bottom of the cage, the Thing scuttled out of its hut. It had arms and legs. It definitely wasn't a snake.

The Thing **GRABBED** the slug and looked into my eyes. So red. There was no way I'd be sleeping much that night. Not with it still there.

CHAPTER 4
The Thing Must Go

I woke up to **thumping** again.

It woke up Josh this time, too.

"What was that?" Josh asked,

peeking into my room.

I was too

scared

to answer.

I just pointed at the closet.

We both saw the door shaking.

Thump. Thump.

THUMP!

"What *is* that?" Josh asked. He reached for the closet door handle.

"Josh! **DON'T!**" I gasped.

Too late.

The Thing BURST out. It looked at us, flapping its wings slowly.

Then it flew right at Josh! Its long TALONS pointed at Josh's face.

Josh **SCREAMED** and

fell. I could see blood through

his fingers.

The Thing flew out of my

bedroom door.

I didn't think. I **RAN**.

Josh was still *moaning*
and grabbing his face. Good thing
Mom was a heavy sleeper.

I heard **heavy**
flapping wings
in the kitchen.
There were
no doors in there. The
window was shut. The Thing would
be TRAPPED. I grabbed a
small trash can and a broom.

The Thing had gotten into our fridge. It sat on the floor, its face in some RAW MEAT.

Its wings were relaxed. I stared at its sharp CLAWS.

I took three slow steps.

The Thing lifted its head and STARED back at me.

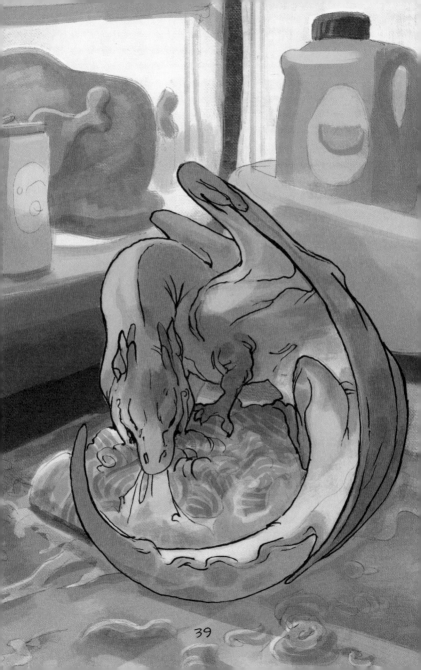

WHOOSH! It flew at my head!

I was ready. I used the broom

like a baseball bat. The Thing flew

into the kitchen wall.

SLAM! I trapped

it under the trash can.

A bandaged Josh helped me get the **THING** back into its cage. We tied a belt around the cage and put it in the trunk of *Mom's* car.

We drove

all the way to

the LAKE.

We carried the cage to the edge of the lake. The Thing looked back at us. Its *eyes* had changed to green.

"Should I let it go?" I asked Josh.

The Thing had attacked us, but I couldn't just leave it to **DIE**.

"Are you crazy?" Josh asked.

I shrugged.

"**Fine**," he said over his shoulder. "You're on your own."

I took a deep breath. "It's not your fault," I said to the Thing. I let it go. It flew straight up. Then it *dove!* I ducked and covered my head. The air around me moved.

When I looked up, the Thing was **GONE!**

The Thing is still out there. Somewhere.

I never went back to see Ms. Fleek. I had to pass  RM. 201 sometimes to get to art class.

I never even looked in her **DARK** room. But I could feel her watching me.